F MONTGOMERY
ontgomery, L. M. ('Lucy Maud')
874-1942.
nne's house of d

D0616996

A DREAM COME TRUE

The night winds were beginning their wild dances beyond the bar, and the fishing hamlet across the harbour was gemmed with lights as Anne and Gilbert drove up the poplar lane. The door of the little house opened, and a warm glow of firelight flickered out into the dusk. Gilbert lifted Anne from the buggy and led her into the garden, through the little gate between the ruddy-tipped firs, up the trim, red path to the sandstone step.

"Welcome home," he whispered, and hand in hand they stepped over the threshold of their house of dreams. . . .

*This edition contains the complete text
of the original hardcover edition.*
NOT ONE WORD HAS BEEN OMITTED.

RL 6, age 10 and up

ANNE'S HOUSE OF DREAMS
*A Bantam Book / published by arrangement with
HarperCollins Publishers*

PUBLISHING HISTORY
*Lippincott edition published 1922
Bantam edition / July 1981
Bantam Classic edition / June 1987
Bantam reissue / September 1992
2nd Bantam reissue / 1998*

"Anne of Green Gables" is a trademark and a
Canadian official mark of the
Anne of Green Gables Licensing Authority Inc.,
which is owned by the heirs of L. M. Montgomery
and the Province of Prince Edward Island
and located in Charlottetown, Prince Edward Island.

"L. M. Montgomery" is a trademark of the Heirs of L. M. Montgomery Inc.
and is used under license by Bantam Books.

*All rights reserved.
Copyright (Canada) McClelland and Stewart Limited, 1922.
Copyright © 1972 by McClelland and Stewart Limited.
Cover art copyright © 1992 by Ben Stahl.
No part of this book may be reproduced or transmitted in any form or
by any means, electronic or mechanical, including photocopying, recording,
or by any information storage and retrieval system, without permission
in writing from the publisher.
For information address: HarperCollins Publishers,
10 East 53rd Street, New York, NY 10022.*

If you purchased this book without a cover you should be aware that this
book is stolen property. It was reported as "unsold and destroyed" to the
publisher and neither the author nor the publisher has received any payment
for this "stripped book."

ISBN 0-553-21318-0

*Bantam Books are published by Bantam Books, a division of Bantam Doubleday Dell
Publishing Group, Inc. Its trademark, consisting of the words "Bantam Books" and the
portrayal of a rooster, is Registered in U.S. Patent and Trademark Office and in other
countries. Marca Registrada. Bantam Books, 1540 Broadway, New York, New York 10036.*

PRINTED IN THE UNITED STATES OF AMERICA
86 85 84 83 82

ANNE'S
HOUSE OF DR.

L. M. Montgomery

With a Biography of
L. M. Montgomery
by Caroline Parry

FOUNTAINDALE PUBLIC LIBRARY DISTRICT
300 West Briarcliff Road
Bolingbrook, IL 60440-2894
(630) 759-2102

BANTAM BOOKS
NEW YORK · TORONTO · LONDON · SYDNEY · AUCKLAND